DESIGNED BY RITA MARSHALL

CREATIVE EDITIONS

HARCOURT BRACE & COMPANY

T H E
WICKED PRINCE

HANS CHRISTIAN ANDERSEN

ILLUSTRATED BY

GEORGES LEMOINE

NCE UPON A TIME,

THERE WAS A WICKED

AND HAUGHTY PRINCE.

His thoughts constantly dwelt on how he might subjugate all the nations of

the earth, and make his name a terror to all men. He ravaged with fire

and sword; his soldiers trod down the grain in the fields; they

put the torch to the peasant's cottage, so that the red

flame licked the very leaves from the trees, and

the fruit hung roasted from the black

and singed limbs.

MANY A POOR MOTHER, WITH HER NAKED BABE, HID AWAY BEHIND THE SMOKING RUINS.

AND THE SOLDIERS SOUGHT HER, AND FOUND HER AND THE CHILD,

AND THEN BEGAN THEIR DEVILISH

SPORT:

THE DEMONS OF THE PIT COULD DO NO WORSE: BUT THE PRINCE FOUND IT ALL TO HIS

LIKING: DAY BY DAY HE GREW MIGHTIER. HIS NAME WAS FEARED BY EVERYBODY,

AND GOOD FORTUNE CAME UPON HIM TO HIS HEART'S CONTENT.

FROM THE CONQUERED CITIES HE CARRIED AWAY GOLD AND GREAT

TREASURE. AND AMASSED IN HIS CAPITAL SUCH RICHES AS WERE

NEVER BEFORE FOUND TOGETHER IN ONE PLACE.

THEN HE BUILT

SUPERB PALACES,

TEMPLES,

AND ARCHES;

AND WHOEVER SAW HIS MAGNIFICENCE, EXCLAIMED, "WHAT A GREAT PRINCE!"—NEVER

THINKING OF THE DESOLATION HE HAD BROUGHT OVER MANY LANDS, NOR LISTENING TO

THE GROANS AND WAILINGS THAT AROSE FROM THE CITIES WHICH FIRE HAD LAID WASTE.

THE PRINCE LOOKED UPON HIS GOLD, LOOKED UPON HIS SUPERB BUILDINGS, AND

THOUGHT, AS FOLKS DID, "WHAT A GREAT PRINCE!" "BUT I WISH TO HAVE

MORE, MUCH MORE! NO POWER IS THERE THAT CAN EQUAL,

MUCH LESS SURPASS,

MINE!"

AND SO

HE WENT

TO WAR

WITH HIS

NEIGHBORS

AND SUBDUED

THEM ALL.

The

VANQUISHED KINGS

HE CHAINED TO HIS CHARIOT WITH GOLDEN

CHAINS, WHEN HE DROVE THROUGH THE STREETS; AND

WHEN HE SAT DOWN TO HIS TABLE, THEY WERE MADE TO LIE AT HIS

AND HIS COURTIERS' FEET, AND EAT THE MORSELS THAT MIGHT BE THROWN TO THEM.

NOW THE PRINCE CAUSED HIS IMAGE TO BE SET UP IN THE MARKET-PLACES AND IN THE

ROYAL PALACES; YEA, HE WOULD HAVE SET IT UP IN THE TEMPLES BEFORE THE ALTAR OF THE

LORD; BUT THE PRIESTS SAID, "PRINCE, THOU ART GREAT, BUT GOD IS GREATER: WE DARE NOT

DO IT." ✎ "WELL," SAID THE WICKED PRINCE, "THEN I SHALL CONQUER HIM LIKEWISE!" AND IN

HIS HEART'S PRIDE AND FOLLY, HE BUILT AN ARTFULLY CONTRIVED SHIP, IN WHICH HE COULD

SAIL THROUGH THE AIR; IT WAS DECKED WITH PEACOCKS'-FEATHERS, AND SEEMED SPANGLED

WITH A THOUSAND EYES; BUT EACH EYE WAS A GUN'S MOUTH, AND THE PRINCE SAT IN THE

MIDST OF THE SHIP, AND, UPON HIS TOUCHING A CERTAIN SPRING, A THOUSAND BULLETS

WOULD DART FORTH, AND THE GUNS WOULD AT ONCE BE LOADED AFRESH. HUNDREDS OF

STRONG EAGLES WERE HARNESSED TO THE SHIP, AND SO IT FLEW AWAY, UP TOWARDS THE SUN.

THE EARTH LAY FAR BENEATH: AT FIRST IT APPEARED, WITH ITS MOUNTAINS AND FORESTS, LIKE

A PLOUGHED MEADOW, WITH A TUFT OF GREEN HERE AND THERE PEEPING OUT FROM UNDER

THE UPTURNED SOD; THEN IT RESEMBLED AN UNROLLED MAP; AND PRESENTLY IT WAS WHOL-

LY HID IN MISTS AND CLOUDS. HIGHER AND HIGHER THE EAGLES FLEW; WHEN GOD SENT

FORTH A SINGLE ONE OF HIS COUNTLESS ANGELS, AT WHOM THE WICKED PRINCE IMMEDI-

ATELY LET FLY A THOUSAND BULLETS; BUT THE BULLETS DROPPED LIKE HAIL FROM THE

ANGEL'S SHINING WINGS, AND ONE DROP OF BLOOD — BUT ONE — DRIPPED FROM ONE OF THE

WHITE PINIONS, AND FELL ON THE SHIP WHEREIN SAT THE PRINCE; IT BURNED ITSELF FAST

THERE, AND WEIGHED WITH A WEIGHT OF A THOUSAND HUNDRED-WEIGHT, AND WITH THUN-

DERING SPEED TORE THE SHIP DOWN BACK TO THE EARTH.

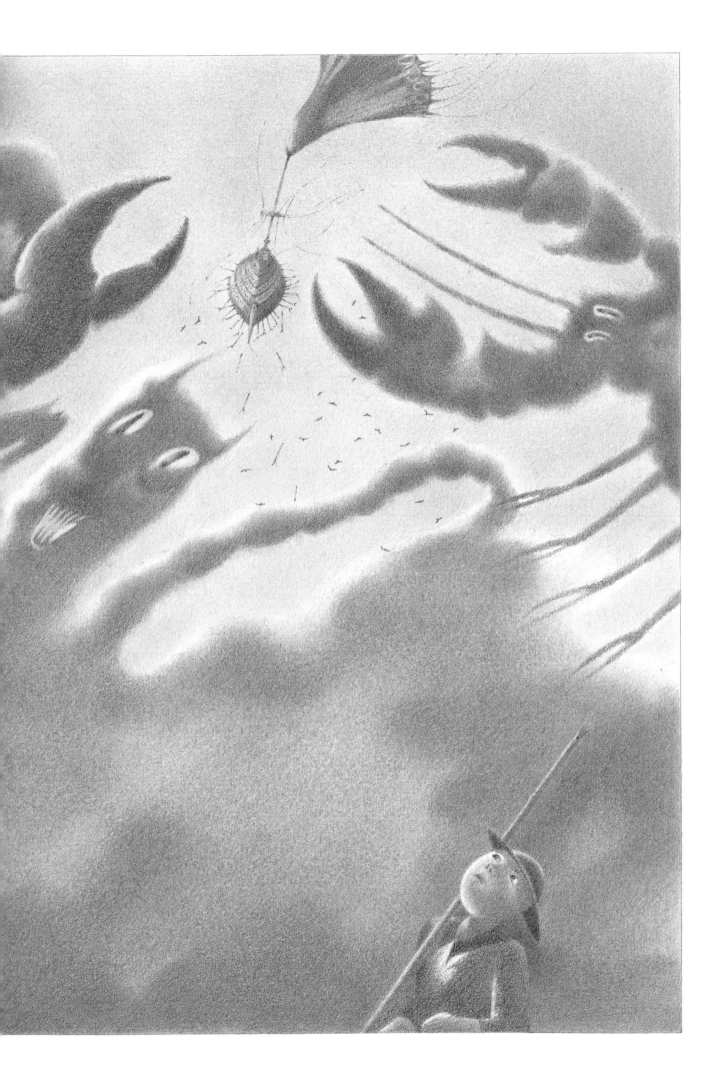

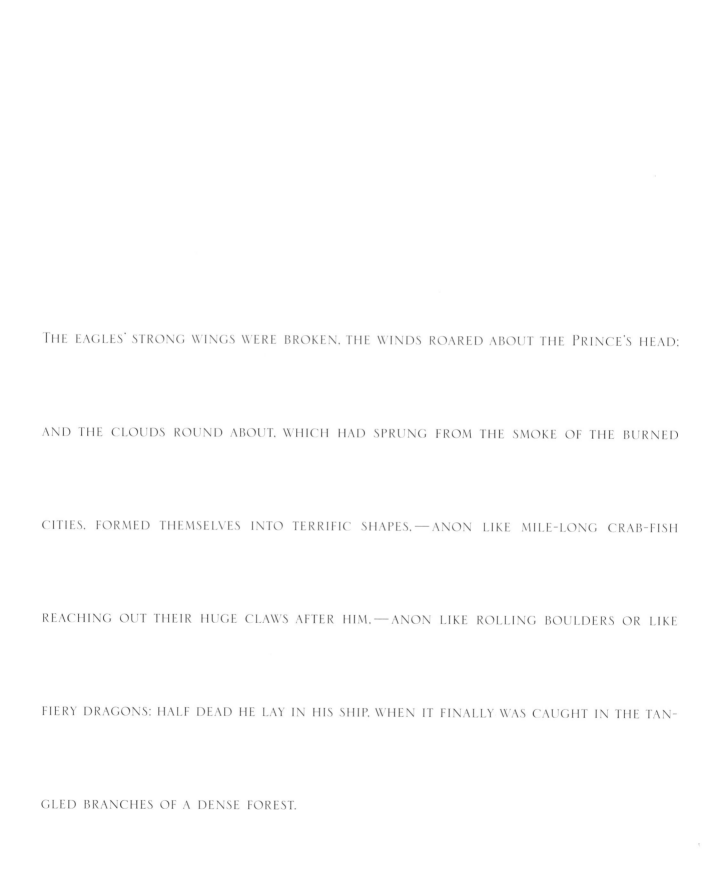

THE EAGLES' STRONG WINGS WERE BROKEN, THE WINDS ROARED ABOUT THE PRINCE'S HEAD;

AND THE CLOUDS ROUND ABOUT, WHICH HAD SPRUNG FROM THE SMOKE OF THE BURNED

CITIES, FORMED THEMSELVES INTO TERRIFIC SHAPES,—ANON LIKE MILE-LONG CRAB-FISH

REACHING OUT THEIR HUGE CLAWS AFTER HIM,—ANON LIKE ROLLING BOULDERS OR LIKE

FIERY DRAGONS: HALF DEAD HE LAY IN HIS SHIP, WHEN IT FINALLY WAS CAUGHT IN THE TAN-

GLED BRANCHES OF A DENSE FOREST.

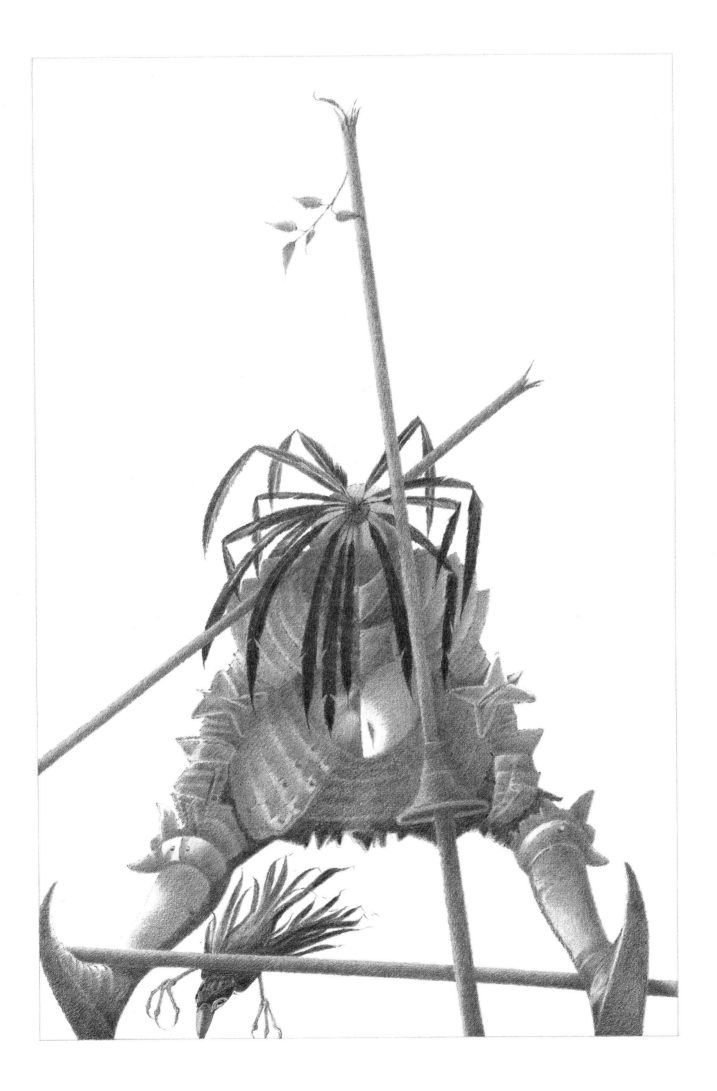

"I *WILL* CONQUER GOD!" SAID HE; "I HAVE VOWED IT, AND MY WILL SHALL BE DONE!" AND

DURING SEVEN YEARS HE BUILT ARTFULLY CONTRIVED VESSELS, IN WHICH TO SAIL THROUGH

THE AIR, AND CAUSED THUNDERBOLTS TO BE FORGED FROM THE HARDEST OF STEEL, WHERE-

WITH TO BATTER DOWN HEAVEN'S BATTLEMENTS. FROM ALL COUNTRIES, HE ASSEMBLED VAST

ARMIES, WHICH COVERED MANY MILES OF GROUND IN LENGTH AND BREADTH, WHEN FORMED

IN BATTLE ARRAY. THEY EMBARKED IN THE ARTFULLY BUILT VESSELS, AND ALREADY THE KING

HIMSELF APPROACHED HIS; WHEN GOD SENT FORTH A SWARM OF GNATS—ONE LITTLE

SWARM—WHICH BUZZED ABOUT THE KING, AND STUNG HIS FACE AND HANDS. IN ANGER HE

DREW HIS SWORD; BUT HE BEAT THE VOID AIR ONLY: THE GNATS HE COULD NOT STRIKE.

WHEREUPON HE COMMANDED THAT COSTLY CLOTHS BE BROUGHT, AND WRAPPED ABOUT HIM,

SO THAT NO GNAT MIGHT REACH HIM WITH ITS STING. IT WAS DONE AS HE HAD COMMAND-

ED; BUT ONE LITTLE GNAT HAD LODGED ITSELF IN THE FOLDS OF THE INMOST CLOTH,

AND CREPT INTO THE KING'S EAR AND STUNG HIM; THE STING SMARTED AS FIRE,

THE POISON FLEW UP INTO HIS HEAD; HE TORE HIMSELF LOOSE, FLUNG THE

CLOTHS FAR AWAY, RENT HIS GARMENTS ASUNDER, AND DANCED NAKED

BEFORE THE ROUGH AND SAVAGE SOLDIERS, WHO NOW MOCKED

THE MAD PRINCE THAT HAD SET OUT TO BESIEGE GOD,

AND HAD BEEN HIMSELF UNDONE

BY ONE TINY

PERMISSIONS DEPARTMENT, HARCOURT BRACE & COMPANY,

6277 SEA HARBOR DRIVE, ORLANDO, FLORIDA 32887-6777.

CREATIVE EDITIONS IS AN IMPRINT OF THE CREATIVE COMPANY,

123 SOUTH BROAD STREET, MANKATO, MINNESOTA 56001.

LIBRARY OF CONGRESS CATALOGING-IN-PUBLICATION DATA

ANDERSEN, H. C. (HANS CHRISTIAN), 1805-1875.

THE WICKED PRINCE/WRITTEN BY HANS CHRISTIAN ANDERSEN:

ILLUSTRATED BY GEORGES LEMOINE.

SUMMARY: IN THIS RETELLING OF A STORY ALSO KNOWN AS

"THE EVIL KING," A VAIN PRINCE DETERMINES TO PROVE HIMSELF MORE POWER-

FUL THAN ALL ELSE, EVEN GOD, ONLY TO BE DEFEATED BY A SINGLE GNAT.

ISBN 0-15-200958-2

[1. FAIRY TALES.] I. LEMOINE, GEORGES, ILL. II. TITLE.

PZ8.A54 1995B [FIC]—DC20 94-45650

PRINTED IN ITALY

FIRST EDITION   A B C D E

DESIGNED BY RITA MARSHALL